Penguin

C000006692

(UN)ARRANGED MARRIAGE

BALI RAI

LEVEL

RETOLD BY PRAKASH PARMAR
ILLUSTRATED BY ALISHA MONNIN
SERIES EDITOR: SORREL PITTS

Contains adult content, which could include: sexual behaviour or
exploitation, misuse of alcohol, smoking, illegal drugs, violence
and dangerous behaviour.

This book includes content that may be distressing to
readers, including descriptions of suicide or self-harm,
abusive or discriminatory treatment of individuals,
groups, religions or communities.

PENGUIN BOOKS

UK | USA | Canada | Ireland | Australia
India | New Zealand | South Africa

Penguin Books is part of the Penguin Random House group of companies
whose addresses can be found at global.penguinrandomhouse.com.
www.penguin.co.uk www.puffin.co.uk www.ladybird.co.uk

 Penguin
Random House
UK

(Un)arranged Marriage first published by Corgi Books, 2001
This Penguin Readers edition published by Penguin Books Ltd, 2024
001

Original text written by Bali Rai
Text for Penguin Readers edition adapted by Prakash Parmar
Original copyright © Bali Rai, 2001
Text for Penguin Readers edition copyright © Penguin Books Ltd, 2024
Illustrated by Alisha Monnin
Illustrations copyright © Penguin Books Ltd, 2024
Cover image courtesy of The Bridgeman Art Library
Design project management by Dynamo Limited

The moral right of the original author has been asserted

Printed and bound in Great Britain by Clays Ltd, Elcograf S.p.A.

The authorized representative in the EEA is Penguin Random House Ireland,
Morrison Chambers, 32 Nassau Street, Dublin D02 YH68

A CIP catalogue record for this book is available from the British Library

ISBN: 978-0-241-63686-2

All correspondence to:
Penguin Books
Penguin Random House Children's
One Embassy Gardens, 8 Viaduct Gardens,
London SW11 7BW

Contents

Note about the story

Bali Rai is an English writer of children's and young adult books. His parents came from the **Punjab*** in India to live in Leicester, England. Leicester is a **multicultural** city, which means that people from many different **cultures** live together in the same place.

(Un)arranged Marriage is about Manny, who also has **Punjabi** parents and lives in Leicester. Manny does not feel close to his family. His **working-class** parents have strong **traditions**. They want to choose his wife for him for an **arranged marriage**, which is normal in **traditional** Punjabi culture. But Manny does not want to marry someone that he has never met before.

(Un)arranged Marriage is about choosing what *you* want to do, and not doing things just because everyone else did them before you. Manny's family want him to be the same as them, but he believes that there are more options in life than just following tradition. He decides to find a way to live the life that he wants.

Before-reading question

1 Read the "Note about the story". What do you know about arranged marriages, and do you agree with them? Do you have arranged marriages in your culture?

*Definitions of words in **bold** can be found in the glossary on pages 92–96.

CHAPTER ONE

May

"No! I'm not getting married."

I was shouting, which I didn't do often. I had come home from school and my oldest brother, Ranjit, was having sex with his wife in their bedroom. I had **ignored** them and gone into the kitchen to get something to eat, but he had come downstairs, saying something about "exercising". I was only 13, but I was not a child and I knew what they were doing up there! It was so **embarrassing**.

"One day, Manjit," Ranjit had said, "you'll be like me – married to a nice **Punjabi** girl and thinking about babies." His wife, Jas, had walked into the kitchen as he was saying it. I just ignored him. I tried to never listen to any of my family.

I hated being called Manjit. It was a girl's name. *Manny* was my name, but my brother still called me Manjit because he knew that I hated it. I was the youngest. I had two brothers. There was Ranjit and then Bilhar, who everyone called Harry. He was 17, fat, hairy and smelly, and he was engaged to a girl who he had never met before. My parents had shown him a picture of a friend's daughter, and he had said "yes" just by looking at her. That was how things were in my family. We had **arranged marriages** as soon as school was finished.

I had two older sisters, Dalbir and Balbir, who were both married and had kids. They lived in different cities with their **in-laws**. In Punjabi families, it is **traditional** for a wife to become a **member** of her husband's family. My sisters had got married to **immigrants** from India, who were working in England and needed the **marriage** to stay in the country. My dad had planned them with friends of his – like doing business. It was so strange to me. How could anyone marry a person who they had never met?

My mum was like a stranger who never spoke to me unless she was shouting at me or calling me for dinner. She never wanted to know how I was feeling.

My dad was always either at work or drunk. He got angry all the time and he shouted at my mum and sister-in-law a lot. Sometimes, he actually hit my brothers, although he didn't do it a lot. They were both turning into men like him and that made him happy.

But he **slapped** me all the time. One time when I **swore** at him, he hit me with a chair. I had to tell everyone at school that I had hurt myself playing football. I didn't care that much about it because he had hit me since I was a kid. I suppose he did it because I was the youngest, or maybe he hated me for some reason. Maybe he could see that I liked **Western culture** more than my brothers. He definitely didn't like my best friend, who was not **Asian**. Getting hit all the time made me feel like I wasn't really part of my family, and the feeling got stronger as I got older.

We lived on Evington Drive, in an area that had a lot of Punjabi families. I had to share a bedroom with Harry because Ranjit and his wife, Jas, took my old room when they got married.

Sharing a room with Harry was awful. He was fat and hairy, left his dirty clothes everywhere and he only showered every three days. At night, I used to go under my blanket and read, but he threw things at me.

"Why are you reading? Are you a *gorah* (white)?"

I hated having no time for myself. Every time I wanted some peace, he was there.

I couldn't even do my homework in peace because my family didn't believe that **education** was important. Quite a lot of British **working-class** Punjabi families think like this. They're only interested in working for money. Ranjit and Harry had both got jobs in factories as soon as they left school and no one in my family cared when I got good exam **grades**.

I spent as much time as possible outside with my friends. My best friend was Adrian – or Ady – who described himself as "Black-Jamaican". Ady and I played football with other boys and we were always together in school, but my family hated Ady. Once, when I was leaving the house, my dad came to the front door.

"Come back, Manjit! Where are you going?" he shouted.

"Just up the road with Ady," I said.

"Ady? Why are you always with that *kalah* (black)? He'll lead you into **drugs** and crime. I know what these *kaleh* do. You'll start stealing and smoking . . ."

And then I got angry and I called him a **racist**. He slapped me and told me to come home before dinner. But most nights he drank so much **alcohol** that he **passed out** before ten and didn't notice if I came home late anyway.

Stealing and smoking? He knew *nothing*. It was actually me who stole first – small things like CDs from the shops in the city centre. It was really easy so Ady started doing it, too. We sold the stuff to other kids at school. We smoked to try to be cool and make the girls notice us.

Ady was a relaxed guy. Nothing made him angry. He lived with his mum and dad, who wanted him to get good grades in school, but Ady didn't do what his parents wanted. He liked to be the bad boy.

I didn't care what anyone said about him. He was my friend and we did everything together.

When Harry got married, I would have to move into a small new bedroom that my dad was building, but this meant having lots of people living in the same house, which I hated.

One of my cousins, Ekbal, who was the same age as me, used to talk to me about it. He was my mum's nephew, but my dad didn't talk to his dad. Ekbal's dad was a doctor and he was the opposite of mine. He was modern and relaxed about things, he believed in education and he wanted Ekbal to go to university. He let Ekbal do what he wanted and he didn't care what colour Eky's friends were.

"Look at him," my dad said about Eky's dad. "Does he think that he's special, with his university education? He's not better than me. I'm a real **Punjabi**, not *gorah* like him."

Why did I belong to a traditional working-class Punjabi family and not a modern one that believed in education? Eky was so lucky.

I sat in my room one night when Harry was playing football with his friends, and I wrote a plan of my life for the next year.

MAY   **HELL** ON EVINGTON DRIVE
JULY   SCHOOL HOLIDAYS – BETTER TIMES?
SEPT   NEW YEAR AT SCHOOL
DEC   RANJIT AND JAS'S BABY ARRIVES – HELL AGAIN
APRIL   THE END OF EVERYTHING
         HARRY GETS MARRIED
         PRISONER IN MY NEW "BEDROOM"
         NO FUTURE

I sat on my bed and read the plan. My life would be finished at the age of 14-and-a-half.

As I sat there, I heard Harry's heavy feet coming up the stairs. I quickly put the paper under the bed as he came in the room.

"What are you doing?" he said, dropping heavily on his bed.

"Nothing," I said.

"Nothing? Mum says you've been up here all day." Then he swore at me and turned on the CD player.

"Swearing is for people who are not smart," I said, which was what my favourite teacher, Mr Cooke, had said to me once.

"Stop talking like you're something special," he said. "Do you think you're some kind of *gorah*? Anyone could think you're white, **innit**."

I hated the way my brothers spoke. Every sentence ended with "innit". They sounded so stupid. I never wanted to be like them.

"You're just a racist, Harry," I replied.

"No, I'm just proud to be Punjabi. You're always trying to be white – that's your problem."

I stared at him. I wanted to kick the stupid racist, but I just called him "daddy's little robot" and left the room before he could throw his **trainer** at me.

———

One Saturday, my dad was getting ready to go to a family wedding. I was watching TV in the living room when he walked in.

"Manjit. Don't you want to come to your brother's wedding?" he asked.

I told him that it didn't matter if I went to the wedding, because it was not really my brother getting married (he was my cousin).

"You young people," he said, "what do you know? Brother, cousin, it's all the same to us. We're Punjabis and **Sikh**, Manjit, not *goreh*, and we're proud of it," he continued. "Ranjit is working and married to a good **Sikh** girl and Bilhar will do the same soon. And when you're Bilhar's age, you'll marry, too."

His age? But Harry was only 17. SEVENTEEN! That meant that I was free for just four more years. Four! This information was like a **slap** in the face. I had plans to be a top footballer, or a famous pop singer, or to write an amazing book. I was not planning to get married at 17 to a girl that I didn't know.

I was staring at the TV, hoping that I had imagined it all. Maybe this was just a horrible dream? My dad stood up and looked straight at me.

"Are you listening to me, Manjit?"

"Yes, Daddy," I replied, trying not to let him see my face. My mouth was getting dry, I was **sweating** and I felt sick.

"Good. I have a friend whose daughter is only a few months older than you. She needs a husband so that she can stay in England. He's my good friend, Manjit, who did me a favour once. But we'll talk about this when the time is better. Not now."

And he walked out of the room. I sat there feeling shocked.

There had to be a way of escaping. There had to be something I could do, like using a **cheat** that you get in computer games. I needed a way to get to the next **level** without getting killed by my enemies. There had to be one, because I could not just stop this game and start again later. This was serious.

CHAPTER TWO

July

The cheat started in July and I began to go a bit crazy. I remember waking up one morning and feeling like I'd had enough of everything. It was a sunny day, the sky was blue and there were no clouds, but I didn't feel happy. I was still feeling shocked by what my dad had said in May, about marriage at 17. His words kept repeating in my mind and I needed to do anything to stop myself thinking about them.

I met Ady nearly every afternoon that summer holiday, looking for crazy things to do. One afternoon, we were walking up Evington Road to the city centre and I was playing a game called "find the white man" because this area was about ninety per cent Asian. Almost all the shops and people were Asian or black. This is why I loved Leicester. It was a mix of everyone and very **multicultural**. My family didn't believe that this was a good thing, but Ady and I thought it was fantastic.

In the city centre, we went from store to store looking for something to steal. As we walked, Ady told me about a girl at school, Sarah, who wanted to go out with him. We were walking up another street when Ady pulled at my arm. He pointed at two blonde girls who were walking towards us on the other side of the road.

"That's Sarah!" he said, excitedly, pointing at the taller

girl. But I was looking at the other one, who had long, **curly** hair and **tanned** skin.

"Who's the girl with her?" I asked. I could not stop looking at her. As they passed us, they smiled.

We didn't see them again that afternoon, but in five minutes I had changed from not being sure about girlfriends to wanting the girl with the curly hair.

———————

August

I had started thinking about the curly-haired girl more and more.

Ady and I had just finished playing football with my cousin Ekbal and his friends. "Let's go into town," I said.

"We always go into town," he replied. "Let's do something else."

"But we might see Sarah again. You won't be happy if I see her and you're not there."

"You're just hoping to see the other girl with curly hair!" he said, and laughed.

But he agreed to go.

We went into the Shires, which was the shopping centre in the middle of Leicester. We were there for about half an hour when I saw Sarah coming out of a clothes shop. I looked behind her and there was her friend, too.

Sarah said "hello" to Ady and smiled at me. I think my face went bright red because Ady and Sarah started laughing. I looked at Sarah's friend, who had gone red, too.

"You're Ady, aren't you?" Sarah asked.

"Yeah. But you know that already."

Sarah smiled again and then turned to me. "So who are you?"

I looked from her to Ady and then to the curly-haired girl. She was beautiful, with green eyes, cool trainers, grey black trousers and a black top. I was so nervous. "Manny," I managed to reply.

"I think we should buy you two young ladies a coffee or something," Ady said. I looked at Ady and then back at the girls, while my hands started to sweat and my heart went crazy.

October

We were back at school and Ady was now going out with Sarah. I had discovered that the girl with curly hair was her cousin Lisa, and she went to our school. I could not believe that I had never seen her before.

When we had gone for coffee, Lisa and I had not said much to each other, and I thought that she might not like me. But Ady said that she was just shy. I wanted to ask her to go out again, but I was scared of saying something stupid. And then, what if she said no? I would be so **embarrassed**.

But, also, what if she said yes? Then we would be doing things like phoning each other all the time, and if my brother or dad picked up the phone, they would murder me. It is stupid, but for my parents the only girl that I could see was the one who I would marry. Some families, like Eky's, were more relaxed about it, but not mine.

December

"I can't believe it took us so long to talk to each other."

Lisa smiled and looked across the table at me. We were having a coffee in the town centre. We had met about ten times since that first day and we really liked each other.

I was hitting my coffee cup with my finger. Lisa pushed my hand away from the cup.

"What's the matter? Do I make you nervous?" she asked.

"No," I replied, quickly, before looking away.

"Is something wrong?" She looked worried.

"It's what I said about not being able to take you home because of my dad."

"Manny, I've already told you that it's not a problem. My parents would have no problem if you came to my house."

"What do your mum and dad do?"

"Mum's a teacher at a school and Dad teaches in a university. You should meet them," she said.

"I'd like that," I said.

Something about Lisa made me tell her things that I had never told anyone else. She knew everything about my dad, like his traditional ideas, that he was a racist and his thoughts about my **friendship** with Ady. I told her about the plans for my arranged marriage when I was 17. I told her that I sometimes dreamed that I was not my parents' child. She took my hand and held it the whole time and listened to me more than anyone else had ever done before.

Being with Lisa made me feel amazing. Every time anyone in my house shouted at me, I just started thinking about her. I felt so lucky. She was the best girlfriend ever and I was much happier with her in my life.

December

I waited in the police station for Ranjit to pick me up. A policewoman had told me that I could go home because I had never been in trouble before. Ady and I had missed school to go to a music shop in the city centre. I had seen a CD that I liked and I thought I was being careful, but a shop assistant had caught me stealing it.

The drive home was silent. Ranjit didn't say anything but I knew that he was **upset** with me.

At home, Harry gave me two slaps across the face and then shouted, "Why are you always trying to damage our family's **reputation**?"

"Shut up! I don't have to listen to you!" I was angry and crying.

"You're not going out with that *kalah* ever again!" Harry shouted, and then hit me again.

I tried to kick Harry, but Ranjit held both my arms and said, "Go to your room, now."

I ran upstairs to my room and Ranjit came in about an hour later. I didn't want to talk to him but he asked me again and again what was wrong. After a while, I started to cry and he put his arm round me. It felt really strange because nobody in my family had done that to me since I was a child.

I let him hold me for a minute until I started to feel embarrassed about crying. Then, I pushed his arms away and shouted, "I'M ONLY FIFTEEN AND I'M NOT GETTING MARRIED AT SEVENTEEN! IT'S TOO YOUNG. DAD CAN KILL ME IF HE WANTS – I WON'T DO IT!"

May

"It's time that you start thinking about your future, Manjit."

My dad's **childhood** had been really **strict**. My grandfather was in the Indian army and he had made my dad and his five brothers run five miles every morning before helping the family in the fields. So my dad believed in being strict, too. When Harry told him about me stealing, he was so angry that my whole family got shouted at, not just me.

It was Sunday. I was watching football on TV but I could feel my dad's eyes on me.

"Manjit, I've spoken to my friend in India about his daughter," he said. I just kept my eyes on the TV. I knew he was talking about marriage. I tried not to listen, but as he talked I began to realize that my dad had already got everything ready. The girl was six months older than me and she would be coming to England to visit in two months!

"I've told her father that you will marry her after next summer, when you're both seventeen," he continued. "When you're married, she'll be able to stay in this country and I'll have my final daughter-in-law."

I wanted to scream and shout and swear at him, but I couldn't even move. My mind was totally confused. My dad noticed my face and started talking again.

"I don't want the other fathers to laugh at me for having a bad child. Your mother and I taught you to be a good Punjabi. You're not different from us. Look in the mirror. You're a Punjabi, not a *gorah*. These people are not the same as us."

He was getting angrier and his face was getting redder.

"And don't think that I'm stupid, Manjit. I've seen the way that you've been changing. Stealing, not studying and smoking. Do you think that I will let you continue? No!"

My mum came into the room and she sat down opposite me.

"Your poor mother has cooked and cleaned for you all your life," my father went on. "Think about your family's reputation when you're out with that *kalah*. Why do you do it? Do you want to kill me? Do you want to kill your mother?"

And my mum started crying, slapping her legs and calling to God, which is what Punjabi women do at **funerals**. I knew that my mum was doing this to make me feel guilty. My dad kept saying that he would take me out of school and send me to India until I said yes. In the end, I started crying, too, because I didn't know what to do. How could I make my parents feel so sad?

I had to get married.

CHAPTER FOUR

June

Two weeks after that afternoon, I was sitting in a classroom waiting for Mr Sandhu. He was a really strict teacher and all the bad kids were sent to him. He walked into the room and sat down in a chair opposite me.

"Well, Manjit," he began. "Would you like to know why I want to see you?"

I didn't say anything. I looked at him and then at the clock above the classroom door. I wanted to go outside and spend lunchtime with Lisa. Our time together was special because it would be difficult to see her during the summer when I was at home.

"I have heard that your school results are dropping," he continued. "Is this true?"

Part of me wanted to tell him that I didn't care about any of this, but my cheat didn't go as far as being **expelled**. "I don't know, sir," I replied.

"Manjit, we both know that you're an intelligent young man. Until last year, you were one of the top students in your year group. I've spoken to your teachers and what they have told me is not very good." He was looking straight at me, but he was not angry. He actually looked more worried.

"How do you mean, sir?" I asked.

"Well, Manjit, for some reason your grades are much lower than before. And I have had to ask myself why?

The work isn't harder and you aren't suddenly much less intelligent than you were nine or ten months ago, are you?"

I didn't answer. What could I tell him? The work was not harder but I just didn't want to do it. I could only think about the arranged marriage and how to escape from it. How could I tell him that? He was Asian, too, and probably the same age as my dad.

"Is there a problem with the work, Manjit, or is there something that you're not telling me about?" he asked.

"No, sir."

He looked thoughtful.

"Tell me, Manjit," he said, "what do your parents think of you and Lisa Jenkins . . .?"

———

Later on, Lisa and I were sitting outside.

"He asked you *what*?" She looked shocked when I told her about what Sandhu had asked me. "How did he know about us?"

"I don't know," I said. "He's probably seen us around school. He wasn't angry, just worried about me."

It sounded amazing but it was true. Sandhu knew that I was having problems at home. He had asked me about Lisa and my parents. When I told him that they didn't know about her, he had laughed and started talking about the **pressures** of being young and Asian in Britain.

"He said that he understood all about the difference in culture," I said. "And the craziest thing is that he's married to a white woman."

"Who, Mr Sandhu?" Lisa looked amazed.

"Yeah," I replied. "He said that if I think it's hard now, imagine what it was like for him in the 1960s."

"I don't have to imagine it. Sometimes, people stare at us when we're together. Aren't people really strange?" she said.

"Some people are just stupid and can't see anything except for what colour someone's skin is," I said.

————

After school, while we waited for her mum to drive us home, I talked a little more to Lisa about the way that my parents believed in arranged marriages.

"They can't make you do something that you don't want to do," she said. "Just keep saying no."

"It isn't that easy, Lisa. The girl that I have to marry is going to *be* here. My dad is saying he'll take me to India if I don't agree, and my mum just cries every time we talk about it."

"So are you going to say yes just to keep them happy?" she asked. "What about what *you* want?"

That was the problem. I knew that I didn't want to be like Ranjit and Harry and get married to a girl that I didn't know. But I didn't know what I *wanted*. And I was also scared that if I said no, my dad would kill me and my mum would kill herself. How could I explain this to Lisa? She would never have to choose between what she wanted in life and her family.

24

"And what about me?" asked Lisa.

"You know how I feel about you, Lisa," I said.

"And you know that I love you, too. But, if you get married, are you just going to leave me?"

I kissed her. "Never."

"Oh, Manny, what are we going to do?"

"We'll just *unarrange* the marriage," I said.

Lisa's mum arrived as we were kissing. I was embarrassed and moved back but Lisa held my hand and took me to the car.

November

I had seen Lisa as much as possible during the summer, and, when school started again, I spent more time with her family than mine. I also started to miss more classes to go into the city centre with Ady.

But then Ady got expelled and the school told me that I would be next if I didn't start coming to my lessons. Lisa wasn't happy about me missing classes, either. I told her about my "cheat", but she wanted me to get good grades and I even got scared that she would leave me. So I started going into school every day.

But it didn't last long. One night, just before my birthday, Ady phoned me to invite me to a party. Could I go? I might get into really big trouble, but I could go out through my bedroom window . . .

"What about the cheat, Manny?" Ady said. "You know, your cheat about being a bad boy so that you don't have to do the arranged marriage? Think about it. You're going to be sixteen soon and you want to show your family that you're not a kid and they can't stop you doing what you want."

Ady was right.

"All right, I'll meet you outside," I said.

The night was amazing. I was still drunk when I climbed through my bedroom window at three o'clock in the morning. I'd been frightened that my dad would catch me coming in, but nobody noticed.

End of November–December

After the night out with Ady, I started being a total bad boy. I didn't get to school until after eleven o'clock the next day. I didn't do any work in the lessons, and on the way home I stole two chocolates for my friends from a shop.

One Monday, Lisa and I were sitting in the school playground.

"Are you all right?" she asked, kissing me on the cheek.

"I don't know," I said. "I still don't know what to do."

"I really hate all this, Manny. I know it's your parents' culture, but it makes you so sad."

"Thanks, Lisa. You really listen to me and try to help me. And so do your mum and dad."

"They love you, Manny," said Lisa.

"I'm really glad we're together. If I didn't have you and Ady, I'd go mad," I said.

"You're too young to have to think about so many serious things all the time," she replied.

I held her hand. "I know. That's what makes me so angry all the time."

"Is that why you miss so much school?" she asked.

"Yeah," I said. "I can't see any reason to study if I just have to get married as soon as I finish."

"It's strange," said Lisa. "My dad and I watched a TV programme about young Asian women whose parents make them get married. I always thought that it only happened to girls. I never realized that young men are **pressured** into doing it, too."

"It makes me so angry that I feel like I want to fight the whole world," I said. "That's when I go mad and do stupid things like stealing, missing school and getting drunk with Ady. I know it's wrong, Lisa, but I can't stop myself."

"Well, I don't like those things, but I understand, Manny."

"I know, that's why I lov–" But then I stopped.

"You nearly said the terrible L word again," she said.

I had nearly said "I love you" a few times, but for some reason I always stopped myself just before saying it. Lisa always told me that she knew how I felt so she didn't need to hear it. But I think that she probably wanted me to say it.

"Can you come to my house and stay on Saturday night?" she asked.

"Why?" I asked.

"My parents asked you to dinner," she said. She looked away from me and when she looked back her face was red. "And they want to talk to both of us."

I was a little confused. I was not sure what she was talking about.

"Dinner should be OK," I said. "But my dad would never let me stay the night."

"Can you tell him that you'll be at Ady's house?" she asked.

"I don't think that the old racist will say yes to that," I replied.

"Please, Manny. It's really important."

"OK, I'll try my best. I promise," I said.

In the end, I told Ranjit that I had an important football game to go to with school, and would need to stay away on the Friday and Saturday night. Ranjit said that it was fine and he even gave me twenty pounds to spend.

On Friday night, I went out with Lisa, Sarah and Ady – and Ady told us some shocking news. Sarah was **pregnant** and he was **looking forward to** becoming a dad. I almost wanted to laugh. I could not imagine Ady as a father at all. I stayed at Ady's place on Friday night for the first time in our friendship. On Saturday, he and I went into the city centre, and he admitted to me that he was actually really scared about the baby. He had not told his mum and dad yet.

On Saturday evening, when I arrived at Lisa's house, her mum opened the door and **hugged** me. She told me to get myself a drink from the kitchen. Lisa was in there. I kissed her and got myself an orange juice from the fridge. Lisa told me that we had nearly two hours until dinner.

"So what do you want to do?" I asked.

"I think that my mum wants to talk to you before dinner," replied Lisa.

"About what?" I asked. Then, Lisa's dad, Ben, walked in.

"Hello, Manny," he said, getting a glass of water for himself.

"Hi, Ben. How are you?"

"Fine. I want to talk to my daughter if that's OK," he said.

"Of course," I replied.

"And I think Amanda is waiting to talk to you in the living room," he said, walking out of the kitchen. Before Lisa followed him, I took her hand and asked, "What do they want to talk about?"

She smiled and replied, "Sex."

Half an hour later, I was sitting in the living room with Lisa's mum – Amanda. I was a bit shocked by what she had said. She and Ben knew about Ady and Sarah, and she said that, as Lisa and I were both now 16, they wanted to talk to us. She asked me about our plans and were we thinking of having sex in the near future? Did we understand how to keep ourselves safe when we had sex? I didn't know what to say. I just got more and more embarrassed.

And then her mum asked about my parents. I tried to explain to her that, in my culture, sex was seen as dirty and wrong and we didn't talk about it. Amanda told me that she was happy that her daughter was with a caring boyfriend like me. Then, she said that she and Ben were going out after dinner, so Lisa and I would have the house to ourselves . . .

March

That first night in bed with Lisa made us even closer. We had stayed awake all night talking about it. When I was with her, it was like my problems just disappeared for a few hours and I felt relaxed and almost happy. But in the real world my problems just got worse. I was missing school all the time and spending my days with Ady. Lisa was working hard for her exams and she continued trying to make me go to school. My teachers had stopped trying to help me except for one who told me to do the exams next year. Lisa's dad said the same thing, but I just didn't want to.

At home, I wasn't speaking to anyone. I just stayed in my room or went out for walks with Ady. One lunchtime, I was at school smoking a cigarette and watching some kids play football when Ady came and slapped me on the back.

"What are you doing here? Are you here to do your exams?" I said, laughing.

"I thought you might want to come for a drink?" he said.

"I can't, Ady," I said. "If I get caught, I'm out of school forever."

"Just tell them that you're sick," he said.

"No, I'll be expelled," I said. "But why do you want to go out for a drink?"

"Because it's my birthday, bad boy."

I could not believe it. He was my best friend and I had forgotten his birthday! Well, I had to go for a drink with him.

I told my afternoon teacher that I had a bad stomach ache and I met Ady outside. We went to a pub down the road. I thought that the barman would not sell us drinks, but he didn't seem to care that we were too young to drink alcohol.

We talked about Sarah's **pregnancy** and Ady's plans to get a job and take care of his kid.

By three o'clock, we were both very drunk. I needed to go back to school for my second afternoon lesson. I had planned to say that I had been in the toilets with a bad stomach, but I can't remember which of us thought it would be a good idea for Ady to come into my class, too. I was starting to feel really sick as I walked into the classroom first and Ady followed about a minute after me. The other kids watched us and started laughing.

"Who are you?" the teacher asked Ady. "Where are your school clothes?"

"I'm not allowed to wear them. It's against my religion," he said, and the whole class laughed even more.

The teacher's face went red and then a student said, "He doesn't even go to this school, Miss."

The teacher looked at Ady and then at me. "Wait here. I'm going to get Mr Sandhu," she said.

Me and Ady looked at each other and got up to leave. As I got to the door, Mr Sandhu walked in. I only remember shouting, "Run, Ady, run," before I **threw up** on Mr Sandhu and passed out.

I woke up in bed at home and it was dark outside. I couldn't remember where I had been – only that I had been with Ady at school and had thrown up on Mr Sandhu. My head felt heavy and my mouth was dry. Suddenly, the lights came on and Ranjit was standing and holding a brown envelope in his hand. He was smiling, but it was not a nice smile.

"Well done. You've **embarrassed** all of us now, innit?" he said.

He threw the envelope at me and left. There was a glass of water by my bed. I drank the whole glass and found my cigarettes. I started smoking one and opened the envelope.

The letter was from school, telling me that my education was finished. I was expelled. I felt like throwing up again. Until then, I had felt sure about what I was doing with the cheat and I had not cared. But now I was scared.

April–May

"You *will* go to India with us. I'm not asking you, Manjit. I'm telling you," said Harry. He was standing in my room holding a cup of tea.

I had not been outside the house alone since the week that I had been expelled from school. I had not seen Lisa or Ady. Harry and Ranjit were keeping me in the house like a prisoner. I was really missing Lisa and starting to feel more and more bored and **depressed**. Only Jas, Ranjit's wife, was nice to me and gave me her small TV to watch. The others had just shouted at me or totally ignored me. My mum cried and talked about killing herself because I was not a good son like my brothers.

That was when the conversations about India started. A few years earlier, one of my cousins had started robbing people's houses and taking drugs. He had been sent to India by my uncle for a whole year to make him good again. When he came back, he was married to an Indian girl and started working in a factory. That was what my dad wanted for me.

I wanted to **run away**, but where could I go? What could I do? I had no money and I couldn't get a job without an education. I felt totally alone.

———

After all that, I suppose that you want to know why I decided to go to India with my family. It was because of a few different things. First, my dad started being really nice to me. He said that I didn't have to go if I didn't want to but it was a chance for the family to spend some time together. He said that it was only a holiday, and I didn't have a job and wasn't going back to school anyway, so why not go? He made me feel that I could choose if I wanted to go or not. He was treating me like an adult, and, if I'm honest, that felt good.

And then one evening Ranjit's wife, Jas, came into my bedroom.

"How are you, Manny?" she asked, smiling.

"All right, I suppose," I said.

"You must miss your friends from school," she said.

I nodded, thinking of Lisa and Ady. Every time I thought of Lisa, I got depressed.

"This holiday to India," she began to say. "It's just a holiday, Manny, honestly."

"What about leaving me there so that I become a 'good boy'?" I asked.

"Manny, you're an intelligent young man. Do you think that your family could keep you there? I promise that that isn't going to happen."

I thought about it for a while. How *could* they make me stay in India if I didn't want to? Also, the way that Jas was being nice to me, thinking about my feelings, made me feel good. It was almost like I was a member of the family.

"I'll think about it," I said.

―――――

A few days later, a letter came from Lisa. I opened it in my bedroom and started reading. Inside, she told me that she missed me and that her parents were worried about me. Then, she hit me with this:

. . . We haven't seen each other for so long and I don't think we will for a long while, will we? So I've decided to go to Australia for the summer to see my sister. I know that I love you but I can't just not see you. I'm sorry if you're upset but you have to understand my feelings. I don't know if I will see you again and you might be married by the time I get back in September. I'm so sorry.

Email me if you can. And if you decide to leave – to escape – my mum and dad say that you can stay with them for a while. Please think about it. I'll really miss you . . .

I didn't finish the letter because I was so upset. I got up, put my music on and then I sat down and cried.

Later that evening, I went down to the kitchen to get a drink because my mouth was feeling dry. Jas was in the kitchen and she smiled as I walked in.

"Jas, what you said about India . . .?"

"What about it, Manny?" She was staring at me now.

"I'll go, but only if you can promise what you said to me the other day," I said.

"I promise," she said.

I went back upstairs and thought about my life without Ady, without Lisa.

CHAPTER SIX

June

When we got off the plane at Delhi airport, the first thing that hit me was how hot it was. I was wearing a pair of jeans, trainers, a T-shirt and sweater, and I immediately wanted to take everything off. Harry and Ranjit had gone to get our suitcases so I waited near the doors with Jas and Harry's wife, Baljit. My mum and dad were talking to a couple who they had met on the plane. I was looking forward to being in India and seeing how different it was from England, but I wished I was with Ady or Lisa or my other friends and not my family.

Outside the airport, we walked towards the bus station. I could see people everywhere. Some of them were travellers but mostly they were **skinny beggars** who were **begging** for money. There were men, women, old people, and young kids who wore little more than **rags**. I felt sorry for them and guilty for being so much richer than they were.

We caught an old bus to somewhere called Kashmiri Gate. My father said that there we could get another bus to the city that was nearest to my father's village. The bus wasn't comfortable at all. It had no glass in the windows and the seats were just wood. The road was crazy.

There were animals everywhere, people kept walking across the road in front of the bus and huge trucks passed right next to the open window. It was awful.

At Kashmiri Gate things got even worse because we could not find the bus that we needed.

"Why can't we just find the **ticket office**?" I asked Ranjit. He laughed at me.

"Are you stupid? They don't have ticket offices here. You just pay the driver, innit."

I looked at him, not knowing what to say. I was shocked. There were so many buses and hundreds of people and beggars around. It was mad. Ranjit pointed to my dad, who was talking to a driver and then gave him some money. Ranjit told me to follow him and we walked to where my dad was standing. My dad had paid the driver to take us privately to the **Punjab**. His bus was just as old and uncomfortable as the last one. I thought that we must be closer to the Punjab now. I turned round and asked Ranjit, who was sitting behind me, how long the journey would be.

"Not long." He smiled. "It'll be about six or seven hours, or maybe eight."

He laughed when he saw my face change. *Eight hours!* I couldn't believe it. I turned to look out of the window at the roads, which were still just as busy and crazy as before, knowing that I would not sleep on this uncomfortable bus.

We finally arrived at a city called Jullundur at one in the afternoon the next day. I was hot, tired, smelly and thirsty.

My dad went to find a taxi and half an hour later we began the final part of our journey to the village where my father had grown up – Adumpur.

On the way to Adumpur, we drove through really flat land. The first houses that I saw were square and box-shaped. I also saw water buffalo standing in water.

The taxi moved slowly through the village because the roads were so narrow. We passed more houses, small shops and a huge Sikh **temple**. My father's home had two floors with a **yard** at the front. I could see that the house had been beautiful once, but it had not been painted for a long time. The first thing that I noticed were the water buffalo **tied** against the wall in the yard. There were three adults and two babies. As we walked across the front yard to the house, a man came out to meet us, wearing the traditional clothes of Punjabi men. I couldn't stop staring at him because he looked just like my dad.

"Manjit, say hello to your Uncle Piara," said my dad.

I looked at my uncle and smiled. He smiled back and hugged me.

"At last, we meet," he said. "Come in, Manjit."

We spent the rest of the afternoon relaxing in the house, resting after our long journey on *manjeh*, which are like traditional beds. It was not much cooler inside and I was sweating a lot. I was really needing a cold drink when the first of my cousins, a skinny boy called Inderjit, appeared with cold bottles of cola.

In the evening, the whole family sat together. The older men drank alcohol and the women cooked outside. Uncle Piara gave me a bottle of beer. I looked at my dad who nodded at me and said, "Drink it, drink it. You're a man now, Manjit, not a boy. There's no problem."

I sat on the *manjah* drinking my beer. While everyone talked, I was thinking about what Ady was doing. Then, I started thinking about Lisa. I was with all my family, but I felt alone and depressed.

CHAPTER SEVEN

July

During the following couple of weeks, I met all the members of my Indian family. There was Uncle Piara and Aunt Pritam, and they had three sons and a daughter. Rana, their oldest son, was 24 and had a wife and two young sons. After Rana was Jaspal, who was 22 and married to a man called Jasbir. Lal, the next son, was 19 and had been married for about a year. The youngest of Uncle Piara's kids was Inderjit, who was 16 like me. He was fun and he told me that he would show me around the village. After Piara there was Uncle Gurvinder, who was married to Aunt Harpal. They also had four kids. Three of them were married and the oldest, Avtar, had three kids with his wife.

Meeting everyone was confusing because I already had a lot of cousins back in England. There was also my father's youngest brother, Jag, who was like the **black sheep** of the family that nobody talked about.

Inderjit looked younger than 16 years old. He was really skinny and his trousers were too big for him. His main jobs around the house were taking care of the cows and water buffalo, which looked hard but he always seemed happy. I went out to the fields with him during my third week in the village and he asked me questions about life in England. I told him about things like shopping centres and football, but it was hard to explain and he just smiled at me and called me *gorah*. His life had been so different from mine. He hadn't even seen an aeroplane yet and didn't believe me when I told him how big they were.

"You *goreh* think we're all stupid," he told me, thinking that I was lying to him.

Then, he took out a packet of some things that looked like **weed** rolled in brown paper and tied together.

"Do you smoke?" he asked.

"Weed?" I asked. My eyes were wide open with shock.

Inderjit shook his head and laughed. "No, no. Not drugs, but we can get those here, too. These are *biri*."

"What's a *biri*?" I asked as he took one out of the packet. He explained that it was an Indian cigarette.

"You smoke these?" I asked.

He looked around to check that none of the family was near before nodding at me. "Don't tell anyone," he said.

Now I laughed. I had hardly smoked since I arrived, but I had brought one of my cigarettes with me to the field. I took it out of my pocket and showed it to Inderjit.

"I smoke these English cigarettes," I said.

"You try one of mine and I'll smoke this," he said to me. I looked at the *biri* in his hands and thought, why not?

"All right, but, if I don't like it, I'm having that one back," I said.

"OK," Inderjit said, as he took a box of matches out of his pocket. I was scared that someone might see us, but he saw me and said, "It's OK, brother, no one ever comes out here except me and Jasbir."

"Does Jasbir smoke?" I asked, and Inderjit nodded, giving me the *biri* that he had just lit. It tasted really strong and I started **coughing** as soon as I tried it. I coughed for about a minute before giving it back to him and taking back my own cigarette.

"It's good, isn't it?" he said, and laughed. I didn't agree but it was good to have a couple of people to smoke with on my holiday.

But, later, I began thinking of home again. I walked out past the fields on my own, lit a cigarette under a tree and thought about Ady and Lisa. I started to cry as I finally realized, after two months, that Lisa was not my girlfriend any more. And I hadn't seen my best friend for so long that I had almost forgotten the sound of his voice.

August

Ranjit, Jas and their kid, Gurpal, were returning to Leicester two weeks earlier than us because Ranjit had to go back to work. I was jealous of them and missing home so much. We had been here for six weeks – a long time. I asked my dad about going back with Ranjit, but he said that there was some kind of problem with our tickets and **passports**. They were in a ticket office in Jullundur and we needed to wait two weeks to get them. As I had already been here for six weeks, two more wasn't that much longer. That's what I said to myself, anyway.

I spent the time with Inderjit and Jasbir, checking on the fields or taking the water buffalo to drink some water. By eleven, it was too hot to work so we relaxed under some trees. In the afternoon, we went back to the village and by five o'clock we were at the house, drinking tea and listening to stories that our fathers told us. Supper was at about seven and by eight it was dark outside. Each night, I asked my dad about the tickets and passports and every time he just laughed and told me to be patient.

During the ninth week of my stay in India, on a Tuesday morning, I was walking towards the house from the fields with Inderjit, and my dad was sitting outside with my uncles and reading a letter. He looked up as I got nearer and called me over.

"Our passports have been stolen from the ticket office," he told me, without looking up. For a moment I didn't fully understand, then suddenly it hit me. We couldn't go home.

I looked at my Uncle Gurvinder, who nodded and told me that what my father was telling me was true.

"People here pay a lot of money for passports. It's a big business, Manjit," he told me.

"But . . ." I didn't know what to say.

"We have to go to Jullundur to manage everything," said my dad, quietly. "Maybe we'll even have to go to Delhi to the ticket office there."

"When? When are we going?" I asked, impatiently. I wanted to leave now, to fix everything as soon as possible. It was hot outside but my body felt cold.

"Piara, your mother and I are going. Bilhar and his wife are going to see her family. You're not needed. We can manage it all without you," he said.

"But I want to go, Dad. I'm bored with staying in the village. I want to see more of India." I looked quickly at Inderjit, who looked a bit upset at my words.

"I know, Manjit, I know," replied my dad, "but we can't do anything to change things now, can we?"

I turned round to go upstairs because I didn't want my family to see me cry.

Later on, Inderjit tried to make me feel better by buying me a cola. I was really thankful because he had little money of his own so I knew that he couldn't really afford it. But, when I said this to him, he laughed and said that he had got the money from my dad. This made me laugh, too, and we shared a cigarette out in a field.

As we were walking back, we saw Harry cleaning his face

with a towel. He was sweating all over his body.

"Try washing yourself, Harry. You might even start liking it," I said. Harry didn't say anything so I continued, "Can't you hear me?"

This time he looked up. I started laughing and told Inderjit about how smelly Harry was in the English summers.

"You think you're so clever, innit?" Harry said. "Try laughing next month when you're still here."

"Well, at least it won't be just me, will it?" I said.

Harry almost started to reply, but stopped himself and stood back. I couldn't understand what made him stop – it wasn't like him to do that – but my dad shouted from a room in the house.

"Bilhar!"

And Harry went inside.

My mum and dad left for Jullundur the next morning with Uncle Piara. Harry and his wife left later that day. The next day, Uncle Gurvinder took us to a place called Anandpur to visit some famous Sikh temples there. The journey would be long because Anandpur was high up in the hills.

"We will be back before your parents return from Jullundur," he said, smiling.

I realized that I was looking forward to seeing another place in India. I searched for my camera and found it in the room where my suitcase was. I noticed then that only my suitcase was there. Harry had taken his with him to his in-laws' and I decided that my parents' suitcases must be in their own bedroom.

Anandpur really was beautiful. We spent most of the day climbing the hills and exploring the different temples, and I took lots of pictures. We drove back at the end of the day in the dark. I fell asleep in the car and woke up back in the village.

CHAPTER EIGHT

"No!"

I was crying as I stared at Uncle Gurvinder and Inderjit.

My uncle held my arms, trying to keep me calm. I kicked my foot out and hit someone's leg, but I didn't care. They had all lied to me. They had agreed together to **trick** me. It was like a computer game when you think that you've killed all the enemies on that level, but there is one left behind you. **Game over**. GAME OVER!

"You all lied. All of you!" I cried.

"No, Manjit, no." My uncle let go of my arms. "We didn't know. They didn't tell us anything."

"That's not true! You all knew! That's why you took me to Anandpur so that I wouldn't know that they were gone."

"No, brother," Inderjit started speaking, too. "We never knew a thing about it, honestly."

I thought about it for a minute then I decided that I didn't care who had known. My dad, mum, Harry, Baljit, they had all tricked me. They had made me believe that they were going to Delhi, but the truth was that they had gone back to England and left me in India.

I wanted to be on my own so I went outside. I was crying and I felt like I wanted to throw up. I closed my eyes and felt my head hurting and my stomach turning over and over. I stood there like that for about ten minutes until I fell over.

Someone, probably my uncle, lifted me and carried me back into one of the bedrooms. I didn't even open my eyes. And then I remembered the conversation that I'd had with Harry on the day that my dad had told me that the passports had been stolen.

"*Try laughing next month when you're still here,*" he had said.

I hadn't understood then, but now his words stayed in my mind, laughing at me and telling me that I had been so stupid. They had tricked me, and I had *trusted* them.

I spent the next few days not talking to anyone and eating my food alone. My uncles and cousins tried to make me feel better but I mostly just ignored them. Sometimes, I went to a small yard at the back of the house where someone had tied a **hammock** between two trees. I started spending most of my days in it, writing in my notebook and smoking. My only visitors were Inderjit and a man called Mohan who was one of the **servants** that worked for the family. My family were of the "Jat" **caste** – the farmers of the Punjab – and like most other Jat families, they had servants from a lower caste.

Mohan had seemed quite pleased to see me. He was happy to have someone to talk to. He was cool, Mohan, getting me cigarettes and telling me stories about his childhood. It was nice to talk to someone with a different experience of India, whose family had never had any money. I asked him about the caste **system** and he always said that some people were born to be kings, while others were born to wear rags. I told him that I didn't agree and that I thought all people should be equal.

"You're right, Manjit," he said. "We're all monkeys in this life." He laughed. Then, he said, "But even in the monkey world there are big monkeys and small monkeys."

"So you're a small monkey then?" I smiled.

Mohan thought about it. "Maybe I am, Manjit."

"Well, I don't think we Jat are better than you because you're a servant. We just have the money and land and that doesn't make us better," I said.

Mohan laughed. "For a young monkey, you're very clever," he said.

———

I got a letter from Jas about two weeks after my parents had returned to England without me. It was the third week of August and I had been in India since the beginning of June. In the letter, she said sorry and she promised me that she hadn't known anything about the plan. She said that Harry had known but Ranjit hadn't. My dad had left me here because he was worried that I might try to run away if I went back to England before my arranged marriage. The wedding was planned for November, the day of my seventeenth birthday, and in September he would send me a ticket to come home, and Ranjit and Harry would meet me at the airport. She also said this:

. . . You received a letter last week that I collected and opened for you, I hope that's OK. It was from your friend Ady. He wanted to know where you were and what was happening. He wrote that he has been trying to contact you all summer.

He gave his new address and he said that a girl called Lisa has been asking about you by email. Is that another friend? Your dad doesn't know that I've written to you so please don't tell him. I feel so guilty that you have been left there alone. You may not believe me but I really miss having my little brother-in-law here to talk to. I'm so sorry about what has happened.

See you in a few weeks.

Love Jas.

Once I had read the letter, my mind was full of thoughts. Had Ady emailed Lisa? Where was she – still in Australia? Was Ady a dad yet? Had he realized that I had been kept in India?

And then I realized that my passport must still be here in the house if they wanted me to go back in September. I decided that I would try to find it, and then I lit a cigarette and thought about Lisa.

I fell asleep but I was soon woken by a loud, deep voice.

"Who's this monkey sleeping in my hammock?"

His voice sounded like I had heard it before. I opened my eyes and I saw a man who was about the same height as my father but with long hair. He was wearing a T-shirt, jeans and trainers. I was confused about why he was wearing Western clothes.

Then, Mohan came towards us, smiling, and said, "Say hello to your youngest uncle, Manjit."

I looked at him without saying anything.

"Yes, I'm your youngest uncle and it's nice to meet you." The man smiled and held out his hand. "I'm Jag."

CHAPTER NINE

The day after I first met Uncle Jag, he left to visit some friends, so I didn't get a chance to talk to him.

I was interested in him, partly because he was the black sheep of the family, who nobody discussed, but also because he was Western in the way he spoke and dressed. So I asked the family about him. Inderjit and Jasbir didn't know much, so they just repeated what their parents had told them. Inderjit said that Jag wasn't proud of his family, didn't help on the farm and spent most of his time in other countries.

"He's not a good man. He has strange ideas about **tradition** and religion," he said.

Then, I remembered hearing a phone conversation that my dad once had when I was about 11. He had sworn down the phone and shouted, "We don't need Jag's dirty money!" When I asked him about it later, he just talked about how Jag wasn't a real man.

"So what has he actually done?" I had asked Ranjit.

"He sent some money to India," Ranjit said, "to buy some land for the family. But he just wants to take it for himself." I nodded but I hadn't really understood. That was the only thing I remembered about Jag, and I hadn't thought about him much since then. But now he was becoming more interesting. He was someone who had not followed family tradition and had done what he wanted to.

When I asked my Aunt Harpal about it, she said, "Jag is a very strange man. We think that he has a wife and children somewhere but no one is really sure. He spends a lot of time travelling and working in places like Australia."

"He seems quite nice, Aunty," I said.

"What you see, Manjit, is only one part of him," she replied. "He can be very nice but also uncaring and **selfish**. When your grandfather died, he didn't come to the funeral or even send a letter."

"Maybe he didn't know?" I said.

"He knew. Your Uncle Piara wrote to him about it."

"But what does he do?" I asked.

"We don't know. He tells no one and no one asks him about it," she replied.

I was very surprised, but decided to wait until Uncle Jag came back so that I could ask him myself.

On the day when I knew that Uncle Jag was going to return, I went to the hammock in the morning. It was another extremely hot day and Inderjit and Mohan had said that they were worried about the fields because there hadn't been enough rain.

But I was glad that they were busy in the fields because I wanted some time alone to think. I needed to write a letter to Ady, to explain where I was and what was happening, but Uncle Piara said no. My dad had told him not to let me send any letters. As I lay there thinking about it, I started feeling very depressed. I think I fell asleep then because when I woke up the sun was above me and the air was dry and hot.

My head was hurting, I was sweating and, when I closed my eyes, I saw red lights. I fell out of the hammock and both my knees hit the ground, cutting them. Blood was running down my legs and I felt like throwing up. I tried to walk to the house but the pain in my legs was huge. When I finally reached it, I heard voices inside. Uncle Piara and Uncle Jag were shouting at each other.

"He's just a child! What is wrong with all of you? Why can't you let people be who they are?" said Uncle Jag.

"Why, so they can be like you?" asked Uncle Piara.

"You don't know anything about my life, Piara."

"And I don't want to," said Uncle Piara.

"I live my life for me. Not you. Not our father. Me!" said Uncle Jag.

"You were always selfish, even when you were a child . . ."

I opened the door, realizing that they were talking about me. They both turned to look at me as I fell against the wall and passed out.

———

"It's called sunstroke, young man. You were in the sun too long," said Uncle Jag.

I was lying on a *manjah* in one of the bedrooms with Uncle Jag sitting beside me. I tried to get up but he pushed me down.

"Keep still, Manjit. Now is not the time to start walking around. Sunstroke can be very serious," he said.

"Uncle?" I said.

"Yes?"

"Can I ask you to do me a favour? Will you call me Manny? I hate being called Manjit."

"Sure, I'll call you Manny. But you have to do me a favour, too," he said.

"What?" I asked.

"Don't call me Uncle. You can just call me Jag. You don't have to treat me with extra **respect** because I'm older than you."

"OK. What were you and Uncle Piara fighting about?" I asked.

"You," he said. "But get some rest and I'll explain more soon."

————

A couple of days after I had passed out with sunstroke, Jag and I were sitting outside drinking sweet tea. It was cooler and the rest of the family were out of the house.

"What do you do?" I asked Jag.

He thought about it, before saying, "Well, I got myself an education and went away rather than stay here and be a Jat."

"So you left here then?" I asked.

"Yes, I went to school here first and then to college and to university in Delhi," he said.

"What about Uncle Piara and Uncle Gurvinder? Did they go to school?"

Jag smiled. "They don't think that education can help

them manage a farm. But it *can* help them. I studied about farms at university and now I work for the Australian government. I can help them, but they don't want my help."

"Yeah, didn't you send them money?" I said.

Jag looked surprised that I knew this. "More than once, Manny, and they just gave it back. I've got more than enough to give them, but making that money wasn't easy. I was working out in the fields when your grandad died and I didn't get the letter for three weeks. I even missed the funeral."

I remembered what my aunt had said about Jag being selfish, but his face showed that he was very hurt about his father's death.

He took a packet of cigarettes out of his bag.

"Do you smoke?" he asked.

"Err no, Uncle, I mean Jag," I said.

"It's OK, Manny. Mohan told me."

"Did he?" I replied. I wasn't very happy at Mohan, who had promised not to tell anyone about my smoking.

"It's OK, Manny," said Jag. "I shouldn't really let you smoke, but you're old enough to choose for yourself."

I couldn't believe it. I was sitting with an older family member and smoking.

"Now, I've spent an hour telling you all about what I do, but you haven't told me anything about your own life," Jag said as he gave me some more tea. "And don't worry about me getting cross with anything that you say. I have an *open mind*."

I took a deep breath – and told him everything, about Leicester, about Ady and Lisa, about my family and about the arranged marriage.

And I told him about the cheat.

————

The rest of the family were back in the evening and we all ate dinner together. Uncle Jag had told me that he would think of a plan to get me back home, so I was feeling much better. It felt so good to talk to someone who understood me and who agreed that my family had done something wrong. I began to believe that my life was my own again. We were sitting outside and eating cooked vegetables and **chapatis**. Jag had come a bit late so he was sitting a little away from the others and I went over to him to talk.

"Did you think about what you were saying before?" I asked Jag.

"Don't worry, Manny. It's all under control," he said.

"And it'll be cool with them?" I nodded in the direction of Uncle Piara.

"Manny, this is about what *you* want, not what they want. You let me worry about what they think, OK?" he said.

I nodded.

"Good, now go and get me a bottle of beer, please, and after I've finished eating we'll go outside and I'll tell you my idea," he said.

I nodded, smiling. What had he planned since earlier in the day? I was ready to get out of Adumpur and out of India. I was ready to go back home to Leicester to find my cheat and go up to the next level.

CHAPTER TEN

September

The plan took just over a week to get ready. Getting my passport was easy in the end. Inderjit had been told by his dad not to tell me where it was. But, while we were drinking a bottle of beer one day, he made a mistake and let me know that it was under Uncle Piara's bed. He was like a scared kid when he realized what he had done, but I told him not to worry. "I'm not going anywhere, am I?" I told him, and he felt better.

Later on, I was relaxing when I heard Mohan working outside. I got up to give him a cigarette.

"No, thanks," he said, taking a *biri* from his own pocket. "I can't start liking your cigarettes too much. How will I afford them when you're gone?"

"I'll send you some," I replied. "Has Uncle Jag told you what we're going to do?"

"He has told me, Manny," he said. "I have made all the plans." He smoked his *biri* before walking up and putting his hand on my shoulder. "I'm happy for you, now that you're going home soon, but I'm sad, too. You're a good friend to an old monkey like me."

"I'm going to miss you, too, Mohan. You've been really kind to me," I said.

"Will you do me a favour when you get back to England?" he asked.

"Yes, of course I will," I said.

"Will you send me some of the photos that you have taken with your camera? I don't have any photographs of my family."

I remembered that I had taken some photos of his wife and kids, and some of his father, who was very old.

"Of course, Uncle," I said. "I promise."

"We have never had cameras," said Mohan. "We're just poor people."

He wasn't trying to make me feel sorry for him. He was just talking about life. I had already decided anyway to give him my camera. Being in India had made me think about everything that I had. I looked down at my dirty old trainers and realized that I was lucky even to have these. Most people in India had nothing. The camera would be ten times more special to Mohan than to me.

Later that evening, Aunt Harpal said to me, "I hear that you're going to make *paratha* for us one morning." She seemed to think that it was very funny.

"*Paratha?*" I said. I didn't know what she was talking about. *Paratha* are like double chapatis filled with potatoes or vegetables.

"Yes, he is," said Jag from behind me. "He wanted me to show him how to make them so that he could say thank you for looking after him."

I stared at my uncle who just carried on smiling.

"Don't worry, Manny," he explained, quietly. "*Paratha* are part of the plan. I'll explain it all later."

The next afternoon, I was waiting outside for Mohan. Uncle Jag had told me to meet him and collect a packet of something. Jag didn't tell me what was in it, but just to take it from Mohan and then get my things ready to go back to England. I had managed to pack my stuff into my rucksack without anyone noticing.

I waited for about an hour before Mohan came on Inderjit's old bike.

"Here is your little present," he said, giving me a brown paper packet. "Don't ask me what it is, Manny. I can't tell you or I will lose my only friend in this family." He was talking about Jag.

"I'm your friend, too," I said, and I turned to the hammock and picked up my camera, my own little present for Mohan. "Here. This is for you."

Mohan looked at the camera and shook his head. "No, Manny, no."

"It's not about that," I answered. "I *want* you to have it, Uncle, for being so kind to me." That was the second time I had called him Uncle. Mohan was from a lower caste than me. It was the tradition that I should not show him the same respect as a member of my own caste, but I did it without thinking.

"Thank you, Manny," he said, giving me a **hug**.

Uncle Jag was very happy when I gave him the packet outside the house later that evening. He handed me a large grey bag.

"Here, take this," he said.

I held it and looked inside. "What's it for?"

"It's for your things. Take it back to the house and put your things in the bottom. Then, fill the rest of the bag with the pieces of wood that we use for fires. I'm going to fill another one with wood, too."

I nodded. "OK."

"After you've done that, put both bags in the **shed**. Ask Inderjit to help you carry them, but don't let him see what you have inside," he said.

"No problem, Jag." I was getting excited now. After waiting and hoping for so long, my last night in Adumpur was finally here.

We walked back to the house. My uncles were sitting and drinking beer and my aunts were busy chopping onions. Some of my cousins were looking after the water buffalo and Inderjit was playing with the younger kids. It was a normal evening in Adumpur except that it was my last one, probably for a very long time.

Just before it got dark, Inderjit helped me carry the two bags outside to the shed.

"So, brother, what are these bags for?" he asked.

"Just some wood to burn some rubbish," I said.

"Rubbish, like what you're telling me now?" he said, smiling.

I looked at him and then at my trainers. "You ask too many questions."

"So they're not for burning rubbish?" he asked.

"No, Inderjit. I'm going to run away back to England tomorrow and the sacks have got all my things in the bottom."

He looked at me with his mouth wide open. I knew what

he was thinking. "Is he lying or telling the truth?" I started laughing and, after a few moments, so did Inderjit.

"I thought you were being serious for a minute, brother," he said, believing my **trick**.

Inside, Uncle Jag told me that we needed to keep the family at home until at least lunchtime tomorrow.

"Because no taxi driver will leave for Delhi in the afternoon," he said.

"How are we going to do that?" I asked.

"We're going to make them *paratha* in the morning," he replied.

I was so confused. "How are *parathas* going to help?"

Uncle Jag just laughed and told me not to worry.

It was dark when I woke up just before three o'clock the next morning. I didn't want to get out of bed when Uncle Jag shook my shoulder, until I remembered why I needed to get up. Then I jumped out of bed. Outside, Jag was starting to cook over a fire.

"There's some yoghurt in the kitchen. Go and bring it with a spoon. And there are some onions and tomatoes in the fridge. Bring those out, too," he said.

I went inside and found everything. When I came back out, Jag was making tea.

"All the adults are going to eat *paratha*, but they're not for the kids – they don't like them anyway so they can have bread and jam. I need you to make that for them," he said.

"No problem," I said.

We gave everyone breakfast at about four o'clock. Uncle

Jag looked after the adults while I gave the kids their food. The adults all liked the *paratha* and **congratulated** us on how nice it was. Because we were the cooks we didn't eat, but Jag fried us some bread to eat after everyone had finished.

By half past four, everyone had gone to start their work for the day. Jag pulled my arm.

"Get your things from the shed and come to the front of the house. Mohan will have a car waiting for us."

My heart jumped in my mouth. It was actually happening. I took one last look around, feeling like I was finally escaping from prison. Then, I got my rucksack out of the sack and went to the front of the house where Mohan was standing with another man in front of a white car.

"So you're actually going?" Mohan smiled.

"Yes, Uncle. I'll miss you."

I hugged him and got into the car, throwing my rucksack in the back. Jag shook hands with Mohan and got in, too, then the car was moving. One minute we were outside the house, and the next we were travelling on the wide road. I started falling asleep as I listened to Jag and the driver talking.

CHAPTER ELEVEN

"I can't believe that you gave them weed! That's just mad."
I was shocked by what Jag had done.

"I only gave them enough to make them sleep for a few
hours. It won't hurt them," he said. "And the kids were with
Mohan's wife so they're OK."

I had woken up about half an hour after we had left
Adumpur. The first thing that I wanted to know was how
we had managed to escape without the rest of the family
noticing. Jag had told them that he was taking me to visit
another town for the day. I didn't know that he had fed
them weed inside the *parathas*. At first, my mouth just fell
open, but then I started laughing.

We arrived in Delhi in the late afternoon and the traffic
immediately got worse. When we got to the airport ticket
office, the people there told us that my plane was going to
leave later than planned, not until tomorrow evening. Jag
booked us a hotel for the night.

———

We had lunch the next day and walked around the city
centre. Delhi was a big city with cinemas, shops and
restaurants. It was much more modern than Adumpur.

"Will you give me your address so that I can write to
you?" I asked Jag.

"Yes, of course I will," he said. "I want to know what you decide to do about your arranged marriage."

I still didn't know what would happen myself. I knew that I didn't want the marriage, but what could I *do*? I had to choose between my family and being free.

Jag seemed to understand what I was thinking about.

"You have to think about what *you* want from life, Manny."

"I know, Jag," I said, "but it's really hard. If I don't get married, my family will never speak to me again. And I'll feel like the most selfish person in the world."

"Trying to achieve your goals doesn't make you selfish. Ask yourself this, Manny. In five years, where do you see yourself? Will you be with a wife that you don't want or doing the things that you want to do, like getting an education?"

I was too young to have my whole life planned for me. Jag had escaped all the traditional stuff and he was succeeding in life. He was right. Deciding what you wanted in life wasn't selfish.

"So are you married?" I asked Jag. "Aunt Harpal told me that you might have a wife."

"Not a wife, a girlfriend called Nancy," he said. "She's a lawyer in Sydney. And there's Mia."

"Who's Mia?" I asked as Jag took out a photo of a blonde woman and a kid who was about four or five.

"She's my daughter. Your cousin," he said.

I was so shocked. He hadn't told me that he had a family.

"You must miss them when you're away?" I asked.

"Yes, I do. But you see, Manny, if I did all the traditional stuff, I could never meet someone like Nancy or have a beautiful daughter like Mia."

I stared at the photo.

"Keep it," he said, "so that you'll know my family when you come and visit me."

The rest of the evening passed quickly. We had a few drinks before going to the airport. We gave each other our addresses and, as the time to leave got nearer, I started to worry more about what would happen when I got home. I tried not to cry as I said goodbye to Jag.

Once I was on the plane, I was so tired that I fell asleep. A few hours later, I was in the airport in England, then on the train and then on the bus heading towards home. Although I was happy seeing all the multicultural shops and restaurants that I hadn't been to in months, part of me wanted to run to Ady's house. But running away was too easy. I had to go home and face my parents. When I finally got to my house, I rang the bell on the door. It was opened by Ranjit. I looked at him and smiled. I wasn't sure what he would say. But he just stared at me and turned away. As I walked inside, my dad came out of the living room.

"So you have arrived then, Manjit?" he asked me. Then, he hit me hard in the face.

PART FOUR: THE WEDDING

CHAPTER TWELVE

October

"Boy, you look darker than me now," Ady said, looking at my tanned skin.

We were sitting in his brother's house in Leicester. I just laughed. It was the middle of October and I had been back for more than a month.

I was working at nights with Ady in a supermarket. The job was not great but I could save some money and spend time with Ady, who was now a father to his son, Zachariah. My family still believed that I would get married at the end of November. I had decided to let them keep thinking that, then I would run away about a week before the wedding. Ranjit and Jas said sorry to me despite not knowing about my dad's plans to leave me in India, but the others were just the same.

"So you're definitely doing the plan?" Ady asked me.

"Definitely, Ady. I've got to do it, for me. I can't live the way that they want me to. Can you see me with a wife at seventeen?" I said.

"Well, look at me, with a kid at my age," he replied. "Anyway, have you seen Lisa since you got back?" he asked.

I looked at him and shook my head.

"Manny, why don't you go and see her mum and ask if she's tried to contact you?" he said.

"I want to, but something stops me, like I'm too embarrassed or scared," I said.

Ady thought about it for a second then gave a big smile. "If you're not going to see her, she's going to see you. We'll go out on Saturday night and I'll tell Sarah to invite her. We'll do it as a surprise. Lisa won't even know that you're coming for a drink, too."

———

I spent the rest of that week working at the supermarket and trying not to spend any time with my family. I was just looking forward to Saturday night, hoping that Lisa would be there. On the Friday afternoon, I was in the kitchen making tea when Ranjit came to talk to me.

"We need to start thinking about the wedding, Manjit," he said. I carried on making my tea and said nothing.

"Daddy has paid for everything. The hall and the food," he continued.

"Great," I said.

He held a piece of paper up to my face. "The whole cost of the wedding is nearly ten thousand pounds, innit?" he said.

"So? I never asked him to spend all that," I replied.

"Listen. I know you're still upset about India but you have to understand. Daddy spent all this money for you. It's your wedding," he said.

"I thought it was yours," I replied.

"Don't try to be clever. I'm just telling you that we're doing all this for you."

I wanted to tell him that I didn't care about money, but I knew that he wouldn't understand.

"I already told you that I'll do it," I said.

"No, you didn't. We told *you* that you'll do it. You just have to agree," he replied. "I don't care what you do after you get married but you *are* getting married. You have to think about our family's reputation." At that moment, a new idea came into my head.

"OK, I'll do it. But, after the wedding, I'm going to do what I want," I said.

"After the wedding, you'll be your own man to live your own life like a good Punjabi," he replied.

I gave Ranjit a half smile when we had finished, but I was thinking about my new plan.

———————

On Saturday night, I met with Ady and Sarah in a bar. While they were talking, I walked around. It was busy and I went to stand outside. After about ten minutes, I felt a hand on my shoulder. I turned, thinking it was an old school friend, and my eyes nearly fell out of my head.

Lisa.

"Hello, stranger," she said.

I didn't even reply. I just hugged her hard and then stepped back to look at her. She looked fantastic. Her hair was shorter

and she was wearing a white top. I just stood there staring at her and holding her hand. And then she started to cry.

I spent that night with Lisa at her parents' house. She told me that she had missed me as much as I had missed her. She had been worried that I might not come back from India at all. Her parents also welcomed me back like I was their son, telling me that I could stay with them if I wanted to. I told them about my new plan. They were a bit shocked, and Lisa was not sure that it was a good idea, but they understood why I was doing it.

———————

Two weeks later, while I was making a sandwich in the kitchen, my dad came in holding some money in his hand. He was drunk as always.

"You're a good boy, Manjit. Here, take this money and buy yourself a suit for the wedding."

"I've got one already," I said, not wanting to take his money.

"No! You have to take it. You've made me proud." He looked like he was going to cry. "I remember when I got married. We couldn't afford a suit so I had to borrow one from my cousin. It was a happy day. The best party of your life is the day of your marriage."

"Yeah, I'm sure it is," I said, but he didn't hear me.

"Here," he said, pushing the money into my hand. I counted it quickly. It was about six hundred pounds, enough to let me complete my plan. I put it in my pocket and said thank you. I felt bad for a minute until I remembered all the slaps and kicks that I had got from him all my life.

I explained my plan to Ady. He was fine with it but he wanted to know why I didn't just leave now. I told him that I needed to do it this way, to show them that I was going to be who I wanted to be.

He understood but he said, "Do what you need to do, but remember that they'll hate you forever for this."

"I know, Ady. And I don't care."

"And you know that you'll never be able to go back?" he said.

I tried to smile but I couldn't. "I know."

"Well, I'm here for you," he said.

"Thanks, Ady."

"No problem."

CHAPTER THIRTEEN

Friday 28th November

"I'm going to tidy my room, to get it ready," I said.

My family were so stupid. They thought that I had completely changed my mind in a few weeks, from not wanting marriage at all to being happy about it now. They liked me again but it was only because I was doing what they wanted. They were not interested in *me*, the person that I was.

Punjabi weddings are usually three days long, with the main **ceremony** on the last day. Today was the first day of the wedding. It was still early, but the house was already full as family members began to arrive. They all congratulated me and told me that I was being a good son and making my dad very happy.

My "tidying" was actually packing my things into black bags and taking them to Ady's place. I told my family that I was throwing away my old stuff before I got married, and they completely believed me.

That evening was the first of the parties. Each one was the same, with the men getting drunk in one room while the women sat together talking in another one. I was going upstairs when Ranjit called me from the living room.

"Oi! Wedding boy! Where are you going? Come and have a beer."

"No, I'm a bit tired. I'll come tomorrow." I was definitely not going to have a drink with them. Instead, I took a walk to Ady's house to discuss the cheat.

Saturday 29th November

I woke up feeling tired on the Saturday morning. Ady and I had drunk quite a lot of alcohol the night before. I got out of bed and opened the curtains. It was sunny and bright outside, but when I opened the window I got hit by cold air. I got my cigarettes and lit one. There were a few family members in the garden but they couldn't see me. I didn't care any more anyway. It was the start of another long day.

At midday, I was watching TV in the living room when my dad walked in with red eyes from drinking so much the night before.

"Manjit, have you bought your suit yet?" he asked.

"I bought it but it's still in the shop," I lied. I planned to buy a suit, but a cheap one because I wanted to save Dad's money for when I rented my own flat.

"When are you going to get it?" he asked.

"In about an hour from now," I replied.

"Do you need some more money?" he asked. I wanted to say yes but for some reason said "no". My dad shook his head and smiled. "Today, you can have anything that you want. How much?"

"No, no. Honest. I don't need any more money," I said.

"Don't be silly, Manjit. This is for your life."

Well, as soon as he said that, something inside me

changed. This was my life? None of this was for me. I had never asked him to arrange a marriage for me. I was trying to stay calm but my face was going red. He didn't notice, probably because he was still drunk from the night before.

He took some money from his pocket and counted about a thousand pounds on the table in front of me.

"No, it's too much," I said.

"Take it, Manjit. I won't ask you again," he said. "Anything that you don't spend you can put in the bank. A married man needs to have money."

I nodded and took the money. Yes, it was going into the bank, but for my new life as a free man. My dad took me and gave me a hug so strong that I could hardly breathe.

"I know things have been wrong between us, but haven't I made you a real man?" he asked.

He was crying. I tried to look away but I couldn't. I started crying, too, not because I felt sad or guilty, but because of everything that he had done to me. And I knew then that I was never coming back.

Sunday 30th November

I got woken up at half past five on the morning of my seventeenth birthday. We needed to leave at about nine o'clock to go to the wedding in a city called Derby. Most of the guests would come on a private bus. It was a tradition in Punjabi families for all the family to travel to the wedding with the boy, to the city where the girl lives.

I got into the car and soon we were on the motorway.

This is when I told Ranjit that I needed to use the toilet. He wasn't very happy about it.

"OK, but hurry. If we're late, we'll make Dad look bad in front of all the guests," he said. "You know how much he cares about his reputation."

There was a toilet near the motorway so he stopped the car there. I got out of the car and went inside. Someone had written the words "Woo Hah" on the toilet door, and someone in the next toilet coughed twice.

We got to the Sikh temple in Derby at about half past ten. As I got out of the car, my dad swore and told us to go to where everyone was already waiting. Ekbal was there and he looked at my suit.

"Your suit looks wrong. It doesn't fit at the back," he said.

"Leave it, Eky. It's fine," I replied.

There were three smaller ceremonies that we had to do outside with the family. Then, we could go inside the temple. When the ceremonies were done, I turned to my dad.

"I need to go to the toilet again," I said to him.

"Again?" he replied.

"I'll be quick," I said.

He told me to hurry. I walked into the temple and asked someone where the toilets were. He told me that they were at the back of the building. I walked through until I found the exit at the other end. I pushed the door but it was locked. I pushed harder but it still didn't move.

It was nearly eleven. There was no time. So I ran at the door and hit it hard with my body and WHAM! The door was open and I was free. I ran down the street behind the temple and looked around. Where was Ady?

As I ran, I pulled off my wedding suit and threw it behind me. I had my normal clothes on under it. A white car drove up from behind and stopped in front of me. Then, the door opened. I walked towards the car and Ady was behind the wheel.

"Your taxi, sir," he said, laughing.

"Where *were* you?" I shouted.

"Relax. I'm here, aren't I? Happy Birthday."

As I shut the door, he drove off down the road.

"Woo Hah!!" he shouted.

CHAPTER FOURTEEN

Tuesday 30th November

It's been two years since I disappeared from the wedding and I feel that maybe I should explain my actions. I'm not sorry for what I did: for the cheat, running away and taking all that money. I still feel that I did the right thing after all the years that my family treated me like they owned me, not like a person.

I'm 19 now and I live at Lisa's parents' house, in her room, but we're not together any more. She's travelling around Asia. She emails me twice a week and I still love her, but in a different way. I had planned to rent a flat but Ben told me to save my money for my education in the future.

I'm still working in the supermarket and waiting to do my school exams. I might have to study at night and work during the day, but I'm happy to do that, because it's something I'm choosing for myself. I'm being the person that I want to be, not the person that my dad tried to pressure me to be.

I haven't spoken to anyone in my family since the wedding that never happened. Sometimes, I'll see Harry or Ranjit in the city centre, but, if they see me, they don't show it. I was scared that they would come to find me and make me go back. Ekbal, who I still see all the time, told me that they wanted to do that for the first few months. But, in the end, they moved away to a different part of Leicester. Ekbal said that no one spoke about me or even said my name. He said that my dad was still just drinking and working, and my mum hadn't killed herself. They were living like before, except my dad had two sons now, not three. I sometimes think that one day they might welcome me back into the family, but, if I'm honest, I know that that will never happen. My family haven't spoken to Jag since he helped me escape. I still talk to him on the phone or email him. Soon, I'm going to stay with him and his family.

The only thing that I feel guilty about is waiting until my wedding day to do the cheat. I was so angry at my family that I didn't think about how it would affect the girl's family. But I still think that my dad has all the wrong ideas about things. People like him only think about traditions and their own reputations. I've been reading about my religion – about **Sikhism** and arranged marriages. The caste system and all the **racist** ideas aren't part of it at all.

As for Ady, he's still as mad as before. He's working with me in the supermarket, Sarah is studying to become a nurse and Zachariah is becoming more like his dad every day. Ady was the one who helped me do the cheat by putting my extra clothes in those toilets by the motorway and borrowing his brother's car to get me.

And then there's me. Things aren't easy at the moment. I have to work hard and be careful with money, but my life is mine now. I've got a new girlfriend, too. She's called Jenny and she's great. We like a lot of the same things, like books and music. She's actually coming here soon because we're going out with Ady and Sarah for my birthday. I don't know what we're going to do, but it'll be fun and I'm doing it because I choose to do it.

And that is what all this stuff has been about.

During-reading questions

1 How does Manny feel about having an arranged marriage?
2 What does Manny want to achieve with his cheat, do you think?

CHAPTER TWO

1 How does Manny feel when he first meets Lisa?
2 Why does Lisa hold Manny's hand?

CHAPTER THREE

1 "These people are not the same as us." What does Manny's dad mean, do you think?
2 Why does Manny decide that he needs to get married?

CHAPTER FOUR

1 Why does Mr Sandhu ask Manny about his parents' opinion of him and Lisa, do you think?
2 Why do people sometimes look at Manny and Lisa when they are together?

CHAPTER FIVE

1 Why is Manny missing school more and getting drunk with Ady, do you think?
2 How does Lisa's letter change Manny's mind about India, do you think?

CHAPTER SIX

1 How does Manny feel on the journey from Delhi to his father's village?
2 Why does Manny's dad let him drink beer?

CHAPTER SEVEN

1 Why doesn't Manny's dad look at him when he tells him about the passports being stolen, do you think?

2 Why does Harry stop himself speaking, do you think?

CHAPTER EIGHT

1 Why does Manny enjoy talking to Mohan?

2 How does Manny feel about the caste system?

CHAPTER NINE

1 How does Manny's family feel about Jag?

2 What is an "open mind", do you think?

CHAPTER TEN

1 Why doesn't Mohan want to accept the camera from Manny at first, do you think?

2 Why don't Manny and Jag eat the *parathas* that they cooked, do you think?

CHAPTER ELEVEN

1 Why didn't the family see Manny and Jag leave the village?

2 What advice does Jag give Manny about the arranged marriage?

3 Why does Manny's dad hit him in the face, do you think?

CHAPTER TWELVE

1 Why doesn't Manny want to contact Lisa?

2 What is Manny's new plan, do you think?

3 What does Ady mean when he says "I'm here for you"?

CHAPTER THIRTEEN

1 Why doesn't Manny want to have a drink with Ranjit and the family, do you think?
2 Why does Manny change his mind about taking his dad's money?
3 Who is the person that coughs in the toilet, do you think?

CHAPTER FOURTEEN

1 Where does Manny live now?
2 Why does Manny's dad now have two sons instead of three?
3 How does Manny feel about his life now?

After-reading questions

1 Was Manny right to take the money from his dad, do you think?
2 Will Manny ever talk to his family again, do you think?
3 How does Manny change during the story, do you think?
4 Manny's life isn't easy at the end of the book. He still has to work and study hard. So why is he happier now, do you think?

Exercises

CHAPTERS ONE AND TWO

1 Complete these sentences in your notebook, using the names from the box.

| Manny | Ekbal | Lisa | Harry | Ady | Manny's dad |

1 *Manny* has to share a room with his brother.
2 .... is going to get married soon.
3 .... is often angry and drunk.
4 .... doesn't really care about studying hard in school.
5 .... has a family who are less traditional and more relaxed about things.
6 .... is Sarah's cousin and goes to the same school as Manny.

CHAPTERS THREE AND FOUR

2 Use these words to join the sentences in your notebook.

| because | while | Despite | so | Although | but |

1 Harry slapped Manny *because* he had been caught stealing.
2 .... his feelings, Manny decides that he has to get married.
3 Manny's school grades are getting worse, ... Mr Sandhu wants to talk to him.
4 Manny doesn't want to do what his parents want, ... he doesn't know what he wants to do himself.
5 Lisa's mum arrives at the school in her car .... Lisa and Manny are kissing.
6 .... Manny tries to be a good student again, it doesn't last long after he goes to a party with Ady.

CHAPTER FIVE

3 **Put the sentences in the correct order in your notebook.**

a .... Ady and Manny get drunk together on Ady's birthday.

b .... Manny decides to go to India.

c .... Ady tells Manny and Lisa that he and Sarah are going to have a baby.

d .... Lisa's parents have an important talk with Manny and Lisa.

e ...*1*... Lisa invites Manny to stay at her house for the night.

f .... Manny is expelled from school.

CHAPTERS SIX AND SEVEN

4 **Which word is closest in meaning? Write the correct word in your notebook.**

Example: 1 – *a*

1 beg	**a** ask	**b** steal	**c** eat
2 skinny	**a** short	**b** thin	**c** small
3 temple	**a** house	**b** factory	**c** church
4 depressed	**a** sad	**b** slow	**c** lost
5 cough	**a** run	**b** walk	**c** breathe
6 passport	**a** document	**b** newspaper	**c** story
7 yard	**a** field	**b** road	**c** garden
8 hug	**a** shake	**b** hold	**c** take

CHAPTERS EIGHT AND NINE

5 **Write the correct verb form, *past perfect* or *past simple*, in your notebook.**

1 I *was* / **had been** so angry after I realized that they had lied to me.

2 They had told me that they were just going to Delhi, but they **lied** / **had lied** and gone back to England.

3 I remembered that Harry **laughed** / **had laughed** about me still being in India next month.

4 Uncle Jag knew that I smoked because Mohan **told** / **had told** him earlier.

CHAPTERS TEN AND ELEVEN

6 **Complete these sentences with the correct words in your notebook.**

passport	chapati	multicultural	selfish
	congratulate	tricks	

To get back to England from India, Manny needs to find his ¹ .....*passport*......, and he is lucky because Inderjit tells him where it is. Inderjit is worried about Manny leaving, but Manny ² .... him and makes him believe that nothing will happen. When they make *parathas*, which are a kind of ³ .... , the family ⁴ .... Manny and Jag on how tasty they are, but they do not know that the *parathas* will make them fall asleep. In Delhi, Jag tells Manny that he is not ⁵ .... for doing what he wants to with his life. When he finally gets back to England, Manny is happy to see the ⁶ .... restaurants and shops of his city, but he is not looking forward to seeing his family.

7 Are these sentences *true* or *false*? Write the correct answers in your notebook.

1 Everyone says sorry to Manny for leaving him in India.
false   No one says sorry to him

2 Manny is not sure about running away from the wedding and his family.

3 Manny and Lisa are happy to see each other again after Manny comes back from India.

4 Manny immediately accepts the money that his dad gives him.

5 Manny tidies his room.

6 Manny takes the money because he needs it for his new life.

7 Manny and Lisa are still friends at the end of the story.

8 Manny's family went to see him after he ran away from the wedding.

ALL CHAPTERS

8 Write the question tags instead of *innit* in your notebook.

1 "Do you think you're some kind of *gorah*? Anyone could think you're white, innit?" *couldn't they*

2 "You've embarrassed all of us now, innit?"

3 "Are you stupid? They don't have ticket offices here. You just pay the driver, innit?"

4 "You think you're so clever, innit?"

5 "The whole cost of the wedding is nearly ten thousand pounds, innit?"

Project work

1 Imagine you are Mr Sandhu in the 1960s. What was it like to have a wife who was white, do you think? Write a letter to your friend, and tell your friend how you feel. Think about the way your friends, neighbours and family are treating you and your wife.

2 Do you agree or disagree with these sentences? Write up to four sentences.

   a It is important to always take our parents' advice because they have more experience of life than us.

   b We should try to follow family traditions as much as we can.

   c Parents and children will always have different ideas about life, so they need to listen to each other more.

3 In the book, you read about Leicester, which is a multicultural city. Look online, and find out about another multicultural city in a different country. Make a poster about why it is multicultural.

4 Write a newspaper report about the wedding at the end of the story. Think about what the different characters might say to the news reporter.

5 Write a letter from Manny to his parents at the end of the story.

An answer key for all questions and exercises can be found at **www.penguinreaders.co.uk**

Glossary

alcohol (n.)
Alcohol is something in drinks like beer or wine. When people drink a lot of it, they become drunk.

arranged marriage (n.)
In an *arranged marriage*, parents choose a wife or husband for their son or daughter.

Asian (adj.)
In the UK, an *Asian* person comes from South Asia (= India, Pakistan or Bangladesh, for example), or their family came from South Asia in the past.

beg (v.); **beggar** (n.)
To *beg* is to ask for money or food because you are very poor. A *beggar* is someone who lives by *begging* for money or food on the street.

black sheep (n.)
If someone is the *black sheep* of the family, they are different from the other *members* of their family in a way that people think is bad or *embarrassing*.

caste (n.)
The *caste system* in India puts people into different groups or *castes*. People of different religions believe in the *caste* system. The richest people are usually higher *castes*, but the poor are usually seen as lower *castes*. *Caste* can affect many things, like which jobs people are allowed to do, and who they can marry.

ceremony (n.)
an event that happens for an important religious reason. Two people get married at a wedding *ceremony*.

chapati (n.)
a kind of flat, round South *Asian* bread

cheat (n.)
something that is usually not honest or fair but helps you to do a thing more easily

childhood (n.)
the time in your life when you are a child

congratulate (v.)
to tell someone that you are pleased about something good that they have done, or that has happened to them

cough (v.)
to push air out of your mouth and make a noise. If you are ill, you sometimes *cough* again and again.

culture (n.)
the way that a group of people from a country, place, religion, etc. usually act and the things that they believe

curly (adj.)
Curly hair is not straight.

depressed (adj.)
feeling very unhappy and without hope, usually because of something bad in your life

drug (n.)
something that people take to make themselves feel happy, excited, etc. Buying and selling *drugs* is against the law in many countries.

education (n.)
a time in your life when you learn things, usually at school, university, etc.

embarrassed (adj.);
embarrassing (adj.);
embarrass (v.)
If you are *embarrassed*, you feel worried about what other people think of something that you or another person did or said. If something is *embarrassing* or *embarrasses* you, it makes you feel *embarrassed*.

expel (v.)
If a person is *expelled* from school, they must leave the school because they have done something wrong, and they must never come back.

friendship (n.)
when two people are friends with each other

funeral (n.)
when people come together to burn the body of a dead person or put it under the ground

game over (phr.)
used to say that it is not now possible to continue or succeed with something you were doing

grade (n.)
a number or letter that a teacher gives to show how good your work is

hammock (n.)
a bed made of thin, strong material. You hang it between two trees.

hell (n.)
Hell is a very bad place. Many people believe that if you are a bad person, you will go to *hell* when you die. *Hell* is also used to describe a very unpleasant experience.

hug (v. and n.)
If you *hug* someone or give someone a *hug*, you put your arms round them to show that you love them or like them a lot.

ignore (v.)
to not care about or listen to someone or something

immigrant (n.)
An *immigrant* comes from another country to live in your country.

in-laws (n.)
relatives by *marriage*, for example the father or mother of your husband or wife

innit (exclam.)
in very informal British English, used instead of "don't you?", "haven't you?", "isn't it?", etc. to change a sentence into a question.

level (n.)
a part of a computer game that someone must complete before they can move to the next stage

look forward to (phr. v.)
to feel happy and excited about something that is going to happen

marriage (n.)
1) After two people marry, they are in a *marriage*. They have promised to love each other and stay together for all of their lives.
2) the time when two people marry

member (n.)
someone who belongs to a group

multicultural (adj.)
having people from many different *cultures*

pass out (phr. v.)
1) to fall asleep because you are very drunk
2) to fall to the ground suddenly because you are ill, too hot, or have had a big surprise

passport (n.)
a document that has your photograph and shows your name and when and where you were born. You need a *passport* to travel to a foreign country.

pregnant (adj.); **pregnancy** (n.)
A *pregnant* person has a baby growing inside their body. *Pregnancy* is the time when a person is *pregnant*.

pressure (n. and v.)
If there is *pressure* from people to do something or people *pressure* you to do something, they try to make you do it by talking, arguing with you, etc.

Punjab (n.); **Punjabi** (adj. and n.)
The *Punjab* is an area in north-west India and Pakistan. If someone is *Punjabi* or a *Punjabi*, they are from the *Punjab* or their family came from the *Punjab* in the past.

racist (n. and adj.)
A *racist* is a person who believes that some races (= groups of people who may share some of the same things, like their history or parts of what they look like) are better than others. Their ideas are *racist*.

rags (n.)
very old, dirty clothes with holes in them

reputation (n.)
Your *reputation* is what people think about you because of the things that you have done.

respect (n.)
You are polite or careful with someone or something that you think is important. You treat them with *respect*.

run away (phr. v.)
to leave a place without telling anyone, because you are not happy there

selfish (adj.)
A *selfish* person thinks only about themselves and does not care about other people.

servant (n.)
a person whose job is to cook, clean or do other work in someone's home

shed (n.)
a building, often made of wood, in a garden or on a farm

Sikh (adj. and n.); **Sikhism** (n.)
If a person is *Sikh* or a *Sikh*, they follow *Sikhism*, a religion that began in the *Punjab* in the 15th century.

skinny (adj.)
A *skinny* person is too thin.

slap (v. and n.)
when you hit someone or something with the flat, inside part of your hand. *Slap* is the noun of *slap*.

strict (adj.)
If someone is *strict*, people have to follow what they say and do what they want them to do. If someone's *childhood* is *strict*, their parents are *strict* with them when they are children.

swear (v.)
past tense: **swore; sworn**
to use rude words, usually because you are angry

sweat (v.)
to produce small amounts of water through your skin because you are hot, ill or nervous

system (n.)
a way of organizing or doing things

tanned (adj.)
Tanned skin is a brown colour because it has been in the sun.

temple (n.)
a building where people from some religions go to talk or sing to God, or to learn about their religion, etc.

throw up (phr. v.)
past tense: **threw up**
If you *throw up*, food or drink that was in your stomach comes out of your mouth because you are ill or drunk.

ticket office (n.)
a place where you can buy tickets for something, for example tickets for a bus or the theatre

tie (v.)
to put a rope (= a long, strong thing) or piece of material round something or someone. You *tie* the ends because you do not want that thing or person to move.

tradition (n.); **traditional** (adj.)
If something is a *tradition* or is *traditional*, it is something that has been part of a group of people's *culture* and ways of living for a very long time.

trainers (n.)
soft, comfortable shoes for sport that people often wear every day

trick (v. and n.)
when you do something that is
not honest to get what you want,
often by making someone believe
something that is not true. *Trick* is
the noun of *trick*.

upset (adj.)
sad or worried about something that
has happened

weed (n.)
a word that people sometimes use
for cannabis (= a *drug* made from
the leaves of a plant. You smoke or
eat it.)

Western (adj.)
Western culture is the *culture* of people
from North America or the countries
in the west of Europe. It is different
from *Asian culture*.

working-class (adj.)
part of a group of people who have
less money or *education* than others
and often work in manual (= using
their hands, etc.) jobs

yard (n.)
a garden. *Yard* is an American word.